The Twelfth Floor Kids

Written by
Ruth Symes

Illustrated by
Nick Ward

The Twelfth Floor Kids

This is Beechtree Flats. The twelfth floor kids live high up on the twelfth floor. Their names are Amy, Dan, Seeta and Eddie.

Meet Amy

Hi, my name's Amy. I live on the twelfth floor of Beechtree Flats with my mum and dad, my twin baby brothers, Nicky and James, and my big sister, Tina.

This is my room. This is a poster of Red Fox.

Meet Eddie

Hi, I'm Eddie. I live in this flat with my mum and big sister, Jess.

Mum and Jess work in Mum's shop in the High Street.

Sometimes I start to make the dinner for when they get home.

I've always lived in this flat. I like looking over the balcony and seeing what's happening far down below.

Meet Seeta

Hello, I'm Seeta. I live here with my dad and mum and two older brothers.

This is my room. I like doing magic tricks and when I grow up I'm going to be a magician. This is my jar of magic star paint. I bought it at the art shop. It's a special sort of paint that glitters when it dries.

Meet Dan

Hi, my name's Dan. I live with mum and my cat, Jinny. My dad lives over the other side of town and sometimes I go to see him at the weekend.

I've had Jinny ever since she was a kitten. When I go to bed Jinny curls up and goes to sleep at the end of my bed.

Meet Jinny

Miaow.

The Lift Monster

told by Seeta

It was on a Friday afternoon when we heard the scary noise.

My friends, Eddie, Amy and Dan and I were walking home from school and were about to go into Beechtree Flats. We all live there, on the twelfth floor.

'It's nearly time for my favourite cartoon on TV,' Eddie said, as we walked through the door.

'I like Superman best,' said Dan.

'Why?' asked Amy.

'Because I'm Superman Dan. I'm not afraid of anything.'

'I bet you're afraid of ghosts,' said Eddie.

'No, I'm not.'

'I bet you're afraid of monsters,' I said.

'Of course not,' said Dan.

I pressed the lift button to go up. But the lift didn't come. I pressed again. Nothing happened.

'The lift must be broken,' said Amy.

'Maybe it's got stuck on one of the floors,' said Dan.

We started to walk up the stairs. When we reached the first floor we pressed the lift button again.
Clonk!

'What was that?' said Dan, looking around.

'The noise came from inside the lift,' said Amy.

Suddenly there was a screeching sound.

'Nee-oow-oow!'

'What *is* that?' I said.

'A ghost?' said Dan.

'Nee - oo - mee - oow!' said the lift.

'Do you think it's the lift monster?' Eddie said.

We'd all heard about the monster that was supposed to live in the lift. But no one had ever seen it. I didn't believe there was one really.

Dan stuck out his tongue at the closed lift door. 'I'm not scared,' he said.

'Yeeooow!' shrieked the lift.

The door slowly opened. We peered inside. I couldn't see anything.

'Neeoow! NEEOOW!'

An orange, furry thing jumped out at Dan.

'Help!' shouted Dan. 'The lift monster is attacking me!'

Then we saw what the orange furry thing was.

'Jinny!' I said.

It was Dan's ginger cat.

'I wasn't scared,' said Dan. 'I was just a bit - er - er ...'

Jinny purred and licked Dan's cheek. The lift door closed and the lift went upwards.

'Oh no,' I said. We'd missed the lift again. *Clonk!*

'It's stopped on the floor above,' Amy said.

We raced up the stairs. Dan was in front. Suddenly he shouted, 'Look out!' and he stopped running. Eddie, Amy and I bumped into him.

'What did you stop for?' I asked.

'A - a - a monster just got into the lift,' he said.

The lift started going down.

'What are you talking about, Dan?' said Eddie.

'There couldn't really have been a monster,' said Amy.

'But there was. I saw it,' Dan said.

Dan quickly looked over the balcony. 'Let's see what comes out of the lift when it gets down to the ground.'

We all watched and waited. A big green monster came out of the lift and walked along the path.

'Look!' said Eddie, pointing downwards.

'I told you I saw a monster,' said Dan.

'Come on,' said Amy, 'let's see if we can catch it.'

'What?' said Dan.

But Amy had already started to run back down the stairs. We followed her. I wasn't sure if I wanted to catch up with the lift monster – not sure at all.

We reached the ground floor and went out of the flats. We ran along the path the lift monster had gone down. But we couldn't see the lift monster anywhere.

'Where's it gone?' said Eddie.

'It's disappeared,' said Amy.

'It's vanished,' said Dan.

We went back into Beechtree Flats. The lift was waiting on the ground floor but none of us felt like going in it. We walked up the steps all the way to the twelfth floor. I rang my doorbell. Mum opened the door.

'I saw a monster in the lift!' I said.

'Did you, dear?' said Mum.

'Wash your hands and then come and have some tea,' Dad said.

'But I saw a monster!'

'Be quick,' said Mum.

When I'd finished washing I tried to tell Mum and Dad about the monster again. They *still* didn't believe me.

'I hope it was a scary monster,' said Mum.

'It was!'

'Was it a big green monster with fangs?' said Dad.

'Yes!'

Mum and Dad looked at each other and smiled. Then Mum said, 'Eat up. Don't forget the Beechtree Flats' pantomime is on tonight.'

After dinner we went downstairs to the social room. There was a stage at one end and lots of chairs had been set out in rows. I saw Eddie, Amy and Dan.

'Did you tell your parents about the monster?' I whispered.

'Yes, but they wouldn't believe us,' Amy said.

'Come and sit down, Seeta,' said Dad.

I sat down next to Mrs Jessop, who lives on the ground floor.

'Hello, dear,' she said. 'I'm looking forward to this year's pantomime. My son's in it.'

The lights were turned off and the pantomime began. It was called 'Big Red Riding Hood'.

Big Red Riding Hood was strong and tough. She wasn't afraid of anything – not the wolf that wanted to eat her, nor the ghost that tried to scare her, nor the monster...

I looked closely. It was a big, green monster. I'd seen that monster before – coming out of the lift of Beechtree Flats.

The green monster growled at Big Red Riding Hood and Big Red Riding Hood karate-chopped it.

'Hi-ya!'

'Ouch!' cried the monster and it ran off the stage.

At the end of the pantomime all of the actors came on to the stage and bowed. I clapped and clapped. The green monster took off his monster mask so we could see his real face.

'That's my son,' said Mrs Jessop. 'Wasn't he a good monster?'

'Yes, he certainly scared us,' I said.

Who did the lift monster turn out to be?

Think of a time when you were scared. What happened?

Birthday on the Twelfth Floor

told by Amy

This morning when I woke up I knew
it was a special day. A very special day
for me. It was my birthday. Yippee!

I jumped out of bed and went to
the kitchen.

'Happy birthday, Amy,' Mum said.

'Happy birthday, Amy,' said Dad.

'Goo goo,' said one of my baby brothers.

'Coo coo,' said the other one.

They're the only words they can say, although they do make other sounds, like giggling and crying *very* loudly.

'Morning, shrimp,' said my big sister, Tina.

Mum and Dad gave me a pair of red roller blades for my birthday.

'Just be careful when you use them,' Dad said.

'I will.'

Mum gave me a parcel wrapped in silver paper. 'This is from your brothers.' Inside was a packet of pink and white chocolate flowers.

'Mmm, thanks,' I said and I gave Nicky and James each a big kiss.

'Here's my present,' said Tina. She gave me a CD of my favourite group, 'Red Fox'.

'Thanks!'

I got dressed. I picked up the roller blades, chocolates and CD and went to show Seeta, Dan and Eddie. I had to press Seeta's bell with my head because my hands were so full. Seeta's dad opened the door.

'She's not in,' he said. 'She said something about going to Dan's.'

I knocked on Dan's door with my foot.

'Sorry, he's not in,' Dan's mum said.

Only one flat left. Seeta and Dan must be at Eddie's. His mum and sister work in their shop on Saturdays.

I knocked on Eddie's door. No one answered. I knocked again and again. I pressed my ear to the door. I could hear laughing. I knocked again, *very* loudly. I felt cross. I knew Eddie, Dan and Seeta were in there. Why were they being so mean?

I went back home.

'What are you looking so grumpy for?' Mum asked.

I didn't say anything.

'Aren't you going to show the other three your birthday presents?' Dad said.

'No.' I went to my room and slammed the door. 'Some birthday this is turning out to be,' I thought.

I looked out of my window and couldn't believe my eyes.

Eddie, Seeta and Dan were walking along the street far below. If they didn't want to be my friends, then I didn't want to be theirs. I listened to my new Red Fox CD and ate a petal from one of my chocolate flowers. I felt miserable.

'Why don't you go and see the others?' Mum called out to me.

I decided to give them one last chance.

I knocked on Eddie's door. Seeta opened it a little way and peered out.

'Hello,' I said, 'can I come in?'

'Sorry,' Seeta said, 'we can't talk to you now, we're too busy.' And then she shut the door!

I stomped back to my flat. This was the worst birthday ever.

Later on, I heard someone knock at our door. Mum answered it and then she came into my room. 'Seeta asked if you'd go next door,' she said.

This time when I knocked on Eddie's door it was opened at once.

'Happy birthday!' shouted Eddie, Seeta and Dan.

'Wow, thanks,' I said. I looked up at a big banner across one wall. 'Happy Birthday' was written on it. There were balloons hanging everywhere.

'It's a surprise,' Dan said. 'We're giving you a surprise birthday party.'

'Come in,' said Eddie. 'We've got loads of food and things for you.'

I went inside. There was a big birthday cake with candles on it and crisps and things.

'I made the birthday cake,' Eddie said.

I was really hungry. We all put on party hats, even Dan's cat, Jinny, had one, and then we ate the food until we were full to bursting.

'Now for my magic trick,' said Seeta, 'I will make a magic scarf just for you, Amy.'

Seeta held up a thin, black scarf. 'First, I paint the scarf like this,' she said, dipping a paintbrush into some clear liquid and washing it over the scarf, 'and then...'

She waved the scarf round and round above her head. As I watched, the scarf that had been plain black turned into a scarf of twinkling stars.

'Wow!' I said.

'For you,' Seeta said and she gave me the scarf.

'Thanks,' I said.

Then we played all my favourite games.

It was the best party I'd ever had and Seeta, Eddie and Dan are my three very best friends.

What was your 'worst birthday ever'?

Trouble on the Twelfth Floor

told by Eddie

My mum and sister like to have a long sleep on Sunday mornings, so I have to be quiet.

After I'd had breakfast I went out into the corridor to see if any of the other twelfth floor kids were out and about. None of them were. I went back into the flat. I was bored.

Then I saw Amy's new roller blades by the door. She must have left them in my flat after the birthday party. I wanted to skate. I could see myself whizzing up and down the corridor. First I'd go fast and then I'd go slow and then I'd go fast again.

Maybe I'd learn how to go backwards and skate on one leg. I'm sure Amy wouldn't mind if I used her new blades without asking her.

I took the blades out into the corridor and put them on. They were a perfect fit. It was difficult moving in them to begin with, but slowly I got used to them.

Skating was brilliant!

Seeta came out of her flat to watch. Then Dan came out.

'You're really good at skating, Eddie,' they said.

I knew I was. I showed them how I could skate backwards.

Amy came out of her flat.

'Hi,' she said. 'What's all the noise about?'

'Look at me,' I said, 'I can skate on one leg.'

I started to skate but something went wrong with the wheels.

'Help!' I shouted as I fell over. 'Ouch,' I groaned. I rubbed my sore elbow.

'My new blades!' said Amy. She didn't care about my elbow, she only cared about her blades. 'You've broken them.'

'I've hurt my arm,' I said.

'My new birthday blades,' Amy said. 'You've broken my new birthday blades.'

I started to say I was sorry but Amy didn't listen.

'Take them off!' she yelled. 'You shouldn't have been using my new blades. I hate you!'

She tried to pull the blades off my feet. It felt like she was trying to pull my feet off too.

'Wait, I'll take them off,' I said.

I pulled off the blades. I didn't like Amy being cross with me, because it made me feel cross with her.

'Here, take your stupid blades back,' I said.

Amy grabbed her blades and went back into her own flat. She slammed the door after her.

Seeta looked at me and then she said, 'I have to go shopping with my dad.'

'I need to go and find Jinny,' Dan said, and he went down in the lift.

I was left alone.

I went back into my own flat. I sat on my bed. I didn't want Amy to hate me. I wanted to be friends. I knew what I had to do. I knocked on Amy's door.

Amy opened it.

'I'm really sorry for breaking your blades,' I said quickly, staring down at my shoes. 'I should have asked you before I used them.'

I looked up.

Amy's face didn't look cross. She was smiling. 'My dad fixed them,' she said. 'My blades are as good as new.'

'Great,' I said.

'Come on,' said Amy. 'Let's go outside. You can show me how to skate backwards.'

Have you ever borrowed anything without asking? What happened?

Twelfth Floor Detectives

told by Dan

'Do you know where Jinny is, Dan?' Mum said, after lunch.

'I'll find her,' I said. I knew where Jinny would be – up that tree again.

Eddie, Amy and Seeta were playing in the corridor.

'Where are you going?' Eddie asked, when he saw me.

'To get Jinny,' I said. 'I think she's climbed up the tree outside Mrs Jessop's flat again.'

'We'll come,' they said.

We went down in the lift together and walked over to the tree.

'There she is,' said Amy, pointing upwards.

The burglar came out carrying a television set. He put it into a yellow van. Then he went back into Mrs Jessop's flat.

Eddie, Amy and Seeta ran back to me.

'I've called the police,' Eddie whispered.

'Keep a watch for them on the corner of the street,' I said.

'Put some of your star paint on his van,' I said to Seeta, pointing to the yellow van, 'and then put some along the path towards Mrs Jessop's flat.'

Seeta poured a trail of the star paint and Amy crept over to Mrs Jessop's open door and put her roller blades outside it.

'Quick!' I hissed as I saw the burglar looking out of the door.

'What're you kids playing at?' he shouted.

Amy and Seeta ran away.

The burglar came out of Mrs Jessop's flat. He closed the door. He didn't see Amy's roller blades.

'Yeeowch!' he shouted as he skidded on a blade and landed on his bottom in the middle of some of Seeta's star paint.

'The police are coming,' called Eddie, running back from the corner.

The burglar got up quickly and headed towards the yellow van. He started the engine and was just about to drive away when the police car screeched to a stop in front of the van.

A policewoman and a policeman got out of the police car. The burglar got out of his van.

'What's going on?' he said.

'Does this TV set belong to you, sir?' the policewoman said, opening the back of the yellow van.

'No, it…'

'We know all about you,' the policeman said. 'You could say you've been marked.'

Seeta grinned. I put my thumbs up. We'd done it. We'd stopped the burglar.

'Marked?' the burglar said. He looked confused.

'Yes, sir,' said the policewoman. Then both of the police officers laughed and pointed to the burglar's bottom. It was twinkling with Seeta's magic star paint.

'Look I didn't steal the TV,' the burglar said. 'I was just taking it to be fixed for my mum.'

Then I looked closely at the
burglar's face. I was sure I'd seen
him before.

'You're the lift monster!' I said.

'You're the green monster that Big
Red Riding Hood karate-chopped,'
said Amy.

'You're not a burglar,' said Seeta.
'You're Mrs Jessop's son.'

'That's right,' the man said.

Mrs Jessop came down the road carrying two bags of shopping.

'Hello, son,' she said to the burglar. 'Haven't you taken my TV to the repair shop yet?'

'No, Mum, the police and these kids thought I was a burglar trying to steal your TV set.'

Mrs Jessop and her son laughed.

I thought the police were going to be cross with us for wasting their time. But one of them winked and said, 'You did the right thing to call us out and I think the chief of police might be very interested in your magic star paint!'

Amy, Seeta, Eddie and I laughed.

'I bet all that detective work has made you hungry,' said Mrs Jessop. 'Why don't we all go inside and have some of the chocolate cake I've just bought?'

What made Dan think Mrs Jessop was being burgled?

What did each child do to trap the burglar?

Which of the 'twelfth floor kids' do you like best? Why?